Hannah Pagett

CW00867082

2P

JESS'S NEW BED

John Cunliffe

Illustrated by Jane Hickson from the Original Television Designs by Ivor Wood

ANDRE DEUTSCH CHILDREN'S BOOKS

Scholastic Children's Books
Scholastic Publications Ltd
7-9 Pratt Street, London NW1 OAE,UK

Scholastic Inc
730 Broadway, New York, NY 10003, USA

Scholastic Canada Ltd
123 Newkirk Road, Richmond Hill
Ontario, Canada L4C 3G5

Ashton Scholastic Pty Ltd
PO Box 579, Gosford, New South Wales
Australia

Ashton Scholastic Ltd
Private Bag1, Penrose, Auckland
New Zealand

First published in the UK by Scholastic Publications
Ltd, 1992

ISBN: 0 590 54045 9

Typeset by Rapid Reprographics, London
Printed by Proost International Ltd

There was an old piece of carpet in the corner of the room, where Jess always slept. But, one day, Pat said, "It's time Jess had a proper bed."

So, when they all went shopping, Pat bought a bed for Jess. It was a basket, with a cosy red blanket in it.

5

When it was bed-time, Pat put
Jess in his new bed.
Jess turned round and round
and snuggled down to sleep.
But not for long. The red blanket
tickled Jess. It made his fur
prickle. It woke him up.

7

When Pat, and Sara, and Julian
had gone to bed, Jess jumped
out of his basket.
Where could Jess sleep?

He crept out through the cat-door. He crept across the fields and into the barn. He made a bed in the hay. He snuggled down to sleep. But not for long. The hay tickled and prickled even more than the red blanket. The mice squeaked and the owls hooted, and Jess could not sleep.

Where could Jess sleep?
He crept out into the fields
again. He climbed a tree. He
found a nice place where there
was a pile of dry leaves in the
crook of a branch. He snuggled
down to sleep. But not for long.
The wind blew and the tree
moved, and Jess thought he
would fall out of bed.

Where could Jess sleep?
He climbed down the tree an
went home again.

He crept upstairs. He crept under Pat and Sara's bed and curled up there to go to sleep. But not for long. When Pat turned over in his sleep, the springs of the bed creaked and groaned. Then Pat began to snore! Jess could not sleep.

15

Where could Jess sleep?
Jess crept downstairs again. He crept into the kitchen. There, by the rubbish-bin, he found his old piece of carpet, where Pat had put it ready to be thrown out the next day. He curled up on it and went to sleep in that draughty place behind the kitchen door.

When Pat woke up, he went to
look in Jess's new bed.
"Where is Jess ?" said Pat.

Then he found him, on the old piece of carpet.

"Poor old Jess," said Pat. "He didn't like his new bed."

"I know what to do," said Julian. "Put his old piece of carpet on his new bed."

"But let me give it a good wash first," said Sara.

And that is what they did.

That night, Jess snuggled down on his old carpet in his new bed. And he was as cosy and comfy as a cat can be.